GREEN WILMA
FROG IN SPACE

TEDD ARNOLD

Dial Books for Young Readers

Specially for
Carmen and Morgan

DIAL BOOKS FOR YOUNG READERS
A division of Penguin Young Readers Group
Published by The Penguin Group
Penguin Group (USA) Inc., 375 Hudson Street, New York, NY 10014, U.S.A.

Penguin Group (Canada), 90 Eglinton Avenue East, Suite 700, Toronto, Ontario, Canada M4P 2Y3 (a division of Pearson Penguin Canada Inc.) • Penguin Books Ltd, 80 Strand, London WC2R 0RL, England • Penguin Ireland, 25 St. Stephenís Green, Dublin 2, Ireland (a division of Penguin Books Ltd) • Penguin Group (Australia), 250 Camberwell Road, Camberwell, Victoria 3124, Australia (a division of Pearson Australia Group Pty Ltd) • Penguin Books India Pvt Ltd, 11 Community Centre, Panchsheel Park, New Delhi - 110 017, India • Penguin Group (NZ), 67 Apollo Drive, Rosedale, North Shore 0632, New Zealand (a division of Pearson New Zealand Ltd) • Penguin Books (South Africa) (Pty) Ltd, 24 Sturdee Avenue, Rosebank, Johannesburg 2196, South Africa • Penguin Books Ltd, Registered Offices: 80 Strand, London WC2R 0RL, England

Design by Nancy R. Leo-Kelly
Text set in ITC Cheltenham
Manufactured in China on acid-free paper
1 3 5 7 9 10 8 6 4 2

Library of Congress Cataloging-in-Publication Data
Arnold, Tedd.
Green Wilma, frog in space / Tedd Arnold.
p. cm.
Summary: Green Wilma the frog is mistaken for an alien child and
taken on a trip through space.
ISBN 978-0-8037-2698-7
[1. Stories in rhyme. 2. Extraterrestrial beings—Fiction.
3. Spaceflight—Fiction. 4. Frogs—Fiction.] I. Title.
PZ8.3.A647Gre 2009   [E]—dc22   2008039497

The artwork was prepared using color pencils and watercolor washes.

jj Fiction

One morning Wilma woke to hear
a buzzing in the sky.

She hopped into the air to catch
a tasty little fly.

An alien family landed,
needing water for their ship.

An alien child came out to play.
He took a little dip.

Finally, Green Wilma's breakfast
landed on the ground.

Carefully she crept up, trying
not to make a sound.

Suddenly the spaceship plucked her
up into the air.

It pulled her in, and then it rose
and flew away from there.

Poor Wilma at the window watched
her little pond retreat.
But then she heard her favorite words:

"I fixed your favorite: Martian bugs,"
the alien mother said.

"But you can't eat until I take
this helmet off your head.

"It must have been the pond water
that turned our Blooger green.

Just get some rest while we turn on
the Health-O-Mat machine."

Robot doctors tried to find out
what the problem was.

And only Wilma noticed a
familiar little buzz.

She chased it all around the room

and out into the ship.

She hopped across the flight controls

and things began to tip.

The spaceship went from warp speed
into boogie-woogie drive.

It bounced off planets, circled stars,
then fell into a dive.

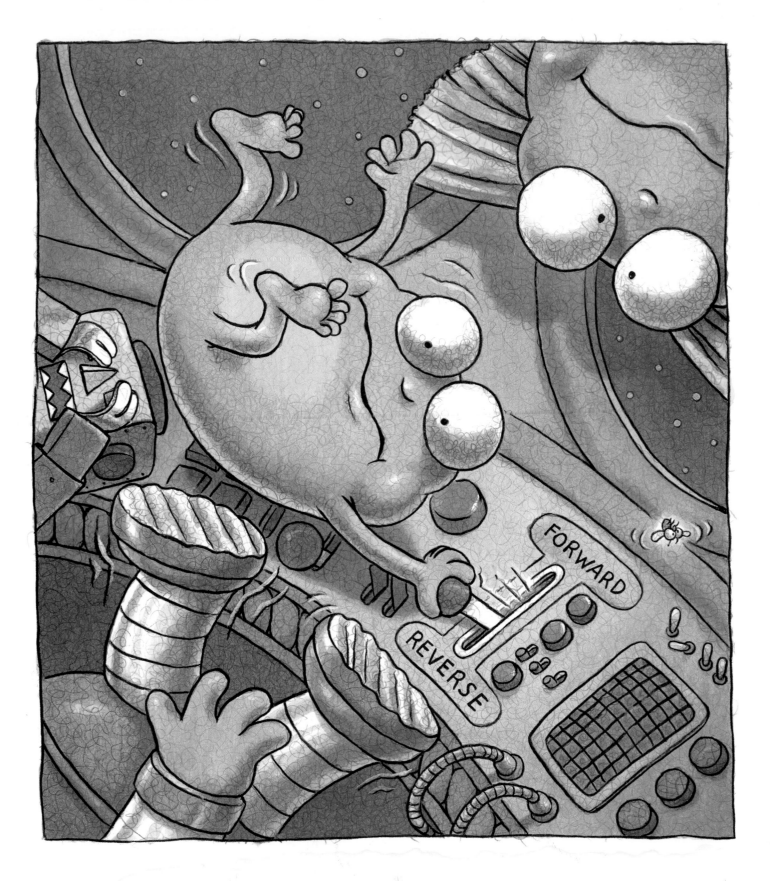

Green Wilma grabbed the nearest thing
and held on to it tight.
The ship flew back the way it came.
Her home rose into sight.

Back at Miller's Pond, poor Blooger
hid inside a tree.
But when he heard a sound he knew,
he hopped outside to see.

Overhead, the aliens booted
Wilma out the door.

They picked up little Blooger and
departed with a roar.

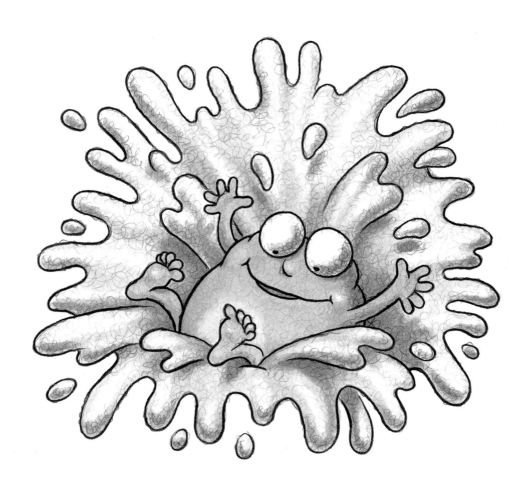

Green Wilma felt quite certain it
had all been just a dream.

No way had she gone up in space
—as real as it might seem!

But what, exactly, was this thing
that shot a pretty beam?